THE UNIVERSE

While You Wait

Cover Design and Artwork

By

James W. McAllister

"Outside of a dog, a book is man's best friend. Inside of a dog it's too dark to read."

G. Marx

Table of Contents

No Duck, Dragon!

The dragon woke up when the hunter stepped on his tail.

"Wha-what? Hey!" The dragon managed a sleepily mumbled non-roar.

"Shh! Be quiet. Can't you see that I'm hunting!" the hunter whispered without turning around.

Osgar rose up, crashing his dragonhead into a branch twelve feet above the short man.

"Ow! Will such indignities never cease?" Osgar grumbled under his breath as he watched the short, balding hunter plod noisily through the forest. Osgar lowered his head, pushing his neck out to whisper in the hunter's ear, "What are you hunting?"

"Rabbit."

That's odd, Osgar thought, "Hey, it's duck season, not rabbit season!" he informed the hunter.

The short, balding hunter spun in an instant and fired both barrels of his shotgun, blowing the dragon's head clean off!

Elmer Fudd was sentenced to 90 days in jail, a $6,000 fine, and 600 hours of community service for hunting dragons out of season.

Life Is Good On Alba

Ahjeld said I should record my story. I do not think it is worthy, but Ahjeld is Maredj of all Alba, so I will do it.

My wife, Rolng, had made the evening meal, as she always did. I had worked a long day in the dudon fields. It is hard work, but it is good for the soul. That is why I chose it.

Rolng always makes wonderful meals. I did not know this when we wed. My father just told me I was fortunate to be paired with her. I thought him so mistaken! Adich was much more pleasing to look at. Alas, she was paired with Nugit. Now, I eat well, and I wake with a smile. Nugit wonders if it is his child that grows within Adich! He laughs at me no more.

These thoughts were in my head that day. I am lucky to be paired with Rolng. When I was ill with the Balonge, she comforted me. When I work hard, I eat well. And when I sleep, she keeps me warm. That night I was planning on being especially tender with her. I raised my hand from the meal to touch her cheek; she smiled and blushed. She is not ugly at all, I thought.

That was when the strangers came, with loud noises and bright flashes. I stood up to see what the commotion was just as one burst into my house. Rolng screamed in surprise. The stranger pointed his little stick at Rolng, and fire leapt out, hitting her chest. I saw the large hole in her, so I asked the stranger, "Why would you do such a thing?" I thought him deaf, or muddle-headed, as he did not respond.

Instead, he pulled me out into the street. Other strangers were there, pointing sticks and burning our homes. They were all grunting very loudly. After a time, I learned to understand their grunts, so I grunted loudly. I believe I said, "Why are you doing this?"

They all stopped and stared at me. One walked up to me and grunted, "We have our orders!"

"Who gave you the orders?" I felt strange. I had never been angry before. I do not like the feeling, so I will try to avoid it in the future.

The stranger grunted at me, and my anger rose. I grunted back, "Show me the one who gave these orders. When my eyes see him, I will make him leave his shell."

The strangers made other grunts then, and dragged me off. Soon, they brought me to their great metal turtle. A stranger walked out of the turtle's belly and stood three heights from me.

"You are the one who ordered this to be done to us?" I grunted.

"I am the Captain of these men. They do what I order them to do!" he grunted in reply.

"Very well then." I grunted. Then pulled him from his shell.

The one who gave the orders fell, his shell empty. The others grunted loudly, and pointed their sticks at me. I sent their sticks away, and they ran into their turtle. Soon it flew away.

I walked home and sat down to finish my meal. Rolng had warmed it for me. She is like that, you know. She smiled as I ate.

I am very lucky, indeed!

Life is good on Alba.

It Came From Outer Space

The crowd gathered slowly at first, but soon the story caught the eye of news outlets, and it was swelling rapidly. Everyone thought it was a good idea to drop their lives and run to see it. After all, alien spaceships didn't land in Onondaga Park every day!

Pretty soon most of the population of Onondaga, Oswego, and Cayuga Counties were there, about four hundred thousand of them. Or as near to "there" as they could get. The ship came down slowly, taking two hours to go from a curving contrail of vaporized water at fifty thousand feet to a large, wide cone slowly descending wide-end first.

Waves of speculation rippled among the crowds. Would they be friendly? Would they be dangerous? Would the ship use wheels, legs, or just sit on the grass? Were the aliens green? Would they have pointed ears? Everyone became silent as the ship settled comfortably upon the grass.

Now, a clear July day in Central New York can bounce an amazing amount of glare off Onondaga Lake. And ninety-five degrees is still hot, even if you do average one hundred and twenty two inches of snowfall each year. The crowd was getting just a little damp; well okay, they were sweating like horses by the time the door opened. You could actually hear the waves lapping on the shore of the Lake, even though it looked flat as glass. No one was breathing.

The alien looked weird. No, not because he had two heads, or long fangs, or glowing fingers: he had none of those. It was his clothing.

Tall enough that he had to duck his head to pass through the door; he stood up and looked at the crowd. Probably in shock; a half million people holding their breaths can't be a common sight in the universe. He reached a long arm, at least, I think it was an arm, up and scratched his head. Yeah, it looked like a head, so....

He turned back into the ship, oh, wait, I didn't tell you about his clothes. He had a thing on his top, it looked like a shirt, so I'll go with that, his shirt was hot pink, with neon green stripes and bright orange dots all over it. His pants, well, there can only be one basic design for something with two legs and a digestive/reproductive port centered between them. His pants were bright yellow on top and bright red on the bottom, with sky-blue dots all over them. And his hat, well, think of a lime-green fedora with a fuchsia feather in it.

So, he turns back to the ship, and yells into it. Squeaks, clucks, and hisses. Some one yells back, and this is repeated three or four times. It sounds like the one still in the ship is getting angry, but they're aliens, so who knows? Finally the alien crosses his arms and starts tapping his foot. After a few seconds, an arm reaches out and hands him a necklace. He quickly puts it on, while rolling his eyes, shaking his head, and mumbling. As soon as it hits his neck, we can all understand him. He was saying, "...telling *me* I should have *known* to bring the translator! And it's not as if I *knew* she couldn't read a starmap! She *asked* to be in charge of the starmap!! Upside down! Yes, *that matters*! Geeze. Ha!"

Well, he's mumbling like this as he walks down the ramp. About half way down he stops, and looks up and across the crowd. Then he speaks to us.

"Uh, er, Hello! Does anyone know the way to, eh, um, Alpha Centauri from here? I'm taking the clan to Meteor World and Asteroid Land this year! All the rides, and the water park, too. Ah, is there a place where I can gas-up the rig, and the wife and kids can freshen-up, and maybe get a bit to eat?"

Well, Heid's was right there, I mean, a no-brainer: root beer, Terrell's chips, and Hoffman's hot dogs. So, I'm pretty sure they'll be back.

All Dressed Up With No Place To Go

"Enterprise, 20 minutes to warp."

"Roger, Control. All systems read nominal. Charlie, you gonna read me a story to pass the time?"

"Ah, that's a negative, Enterprise. Dave, you're on your own. You have fifteen minutes, you could write your life's story!"

"Very funny, Chuck. Did you check the warp comm?"

"Warp comm checks out. Destination coordinates confirmed as midway between Earth and Mars. It all looks perfect, Dave. Relax."

"Yeah, well, would YOU be able to relax if you'd been 'volunteered' to be the first man shoved out of the universe!"

"It wasn't my idea, Dave. Some committee, I think, decided we would send an astronaut on the third warp-drive test. You got volunteered. Think of it this way, you'll be the first man to see nothing!"

"Well, I signed up for it, so I can't bitch too much. Has anyone found or heard from Yang?"

"No, and the CIA is having a conniption fit. They're all in on a turf war with the NASA, DHS, and the FBI. All three are so wrapped up claiming jurisdiction that no one seems to be looking for him."

"Probably not a great idea to put a Red Chinese exchange

scientist on this project. Doesn't surprise me that he's disappeared. Remember how he made multiple back-ups of all that data? It's most likely in Peking by now."

"Two minutes, Dave. Have you heard where Yang was last seen?"

"I think he was in the cockpit here, running another back up. Then he left for dinner, he said. Maybe he warped out!"

"Heh! Not likely. Give me your field read-outs."

"Field integrity 100%. Power reserve plus 80. A little fluctuation on the coil controls, but still within limits."

"They've never fluctuated at all before. Should I delay?"

"No, it's still within limits."

"OK, it's your call. You ready to 'Go Where No Man Has...'"

"Ha, ha, funny man! Final preps. All lights green here."

"All green here as well. How's that coil fluctuation?"

"No change. Looks good."

"Ready for warp, on your mark."

"Roger, warp on my mark. 5. 4. 3. 2. WARP!"

"Charlie, come in!"

"Dave, the warp!"

"Coils failed. Field wouldn't shut down. I'm stuck in warp! Yang must have done something!"

"The warp field, Dave, it's still expanding! The fabric of space, it's disintegrating! The moon's gone! The......."

"Chuck! Come in! Control! ANYONE!"

We're Not in Kansas

I wake in a cold, sweaty shiver.

The nightmare is always the same. Like I have no choice.

I am at the control panel, carefully making the delicate adjustments. To my right, a wall of some transparent material, not quite glass. Behind that, the Survivors.

In front of me is the surgical suite. I have no idea if *they* called it that, but it's all I can think of.

To my left is another transparent wall, but it seems thicker. *IT* sits there.

Waiting...

I have to concentrate, to do this correctly. I don't have any surgical training, so why it's making me do this, I can't say.

My hands shake. I wipe the sweat from my brow as another shiver ripples through me. I feel light-headed, like I need sugar.

I have to concentrate! A little higher up on the leg...there. I adjust the controls, and the incision is made. I can see the boy's mouth open, but my ears don't hear his screams. But I do...

This is the boy's fourth surgery. It takes only a few minutes to remove his leg. The automation dresses the boy's stump and quickly returns him to the Survivors room as a mechanical arm picks the limb off the table. I can't stop watching it. The toes are twitching.

As the dripping limb moves out of sight, I notice *IT* moving on my left. *IT* is excited, pacing in circles, eyes burning.

The boy's leg appears, still steaming. When *IT* jumps up, the mechanical arm releases the severed flesh. *IT* chomps twice and swallows.

The dream is always the same.

It has been for fifty nights now.

At least, I think they're nights.

I remember everyone on the bus screaming when the dark billows engulfed us.

The next thing I remember is being here.

As bad as the nightmares are, I wish I wouldn't ever wake up. Maybe next time I won't. I can only hope.

They took the biggest ones first. Or, they took one of their arms. Then they put them back, and took another. One about every four hours.

After they'd taken the high school kids' arms, they took the smaller kids.

Whole.

Then they took my left leg.

Then the high school kids' left legs.

Then they took my right leg.

Then they took their right legs.

Then they took my arms, both at once.

Then they took what was left of the kids. Torsos screaming

until *IT* chomped on them.

I look to my left, then my right.

I'm all alone now…

The Portal

I moved through the portal horizon quickly. The alien world immediately bombarded my senses with obnoxious sounds, revolting odors, and a fading twilight that cast an odd red tint on everything.

My first order of business was to get out of the open. Quietly I moved behind a large stone block, where I could observe the aliens less conspicuously. Scanning the area, I saw none of the intelligent natives, so I looked closely at the carved stone before me.

This huge block was carved with a combination of decorative designs and patterned glyphs, most likely some form of writing. A few representations of what resembled native wildlife adorned the obelisk, but I could make no logical sense of them.

Nearby a commotion stole my attention. A native intelligent! As the being walked past, I was astonished at how much like me it looked, other than being cast in that dark red tint that colored this world. By the manner of bearing I decided this must be a male, likely of high ranking, so I stepped out to introduce myself.

"Hello. I am Evmor. I have come through a dimensional portal from another world to meet intelligent life," my telepathic greeting was well rehearsed.

The being just stared at me for a short time. His head tilted to one side, and he moved closer. I probed gently into his mind, but I found almost no thought there. As he came within touching range, he let out a loud screech and ran at me.

I had no choice but to shoot him before he attacked me.

The blast attracted the attention of the local fauna. Most of these were huge bipedal things, adorned with various colors. One of them ran right at me, so I had to shoot it, too. The blast burned all of the flesh from its head; the structure revealed looked just like the carvings on the obelisk next to me! What kind of crazed world is this?

More of the huge wildlife came towards me, so I took flight from the area. Soon I found a group of the intelligent beings, and again sought to make contact. But they were like the others, thinking only simple thoughts of food, safety, position, and sex. I left them and tried several other groups, with the same results.

So I went back to the stones, and activated the portal to return home.

But, Whatever Happened To Oliver?

The two humans walked into my shop that Tuesday. I could smell them as they walked down the market; humans have such a distinctive smell.

I had never met a human before. This seemed to be a mated pair, from what I had picked up about human culture. You see, humans are pretty rare these days.

Some give humans the powers of legend and lore. These two just looked like, well, tourists. Well-off tourists, at that.

My shop is nothing special I guess. Just some of this and some of that, curiosities from nearby worlds I buy from a few trader contacts. Occasionally I make a very good buy and have a little more currency. Not often enough to get rich, but I do get by well enough.

"Greetings! I am Achsmel. Welcome to my shop! How may I serve you today?" It is my standard greeting to strangers.

"Achsmel, pleased to meet you. I am Sam, and this is my wife, Alice. We were looking for a Wolf's Eye Fire Stone. Would you have any on hand?" the taller of the humans asked. Very polite, these humans.

"Yes! Yes, I have several! Is there a particular size or color you require?"

"Well, I think green is best for our purposes. Don't you think so, Dear?" the shorter, long-haired one said.

"Yes, I believe you are right, Alice. Green, please, Mr. Achsmel, about 6 carats, if you have it."

"I do! I have several! Here, step this way and let me show you." I led the pair to my gem counter. I had several green Tolrando rubies, which are nearly indistinguishable from green Wolf's Eye Fire Stones, and much less dear, but something told me not to follow that path with these two. So, I showed them the real thing.

"Here you are, sir. There are several here that should fulfill your needs. Do you see one that you like?"

"This one will do nicely. Uh, What is your price, sir?"

"Hmmm, I can let you have it for, oh, say 4,000 credits?" Humans have a reputation as fierce bargainers. So I tried to set my price high enough to give me some profit after he haggled me down, but not so high as to scare him off. I doubled my standard price.

"Done! Here are your credits, Achsmel! A pleasure meeting you, sir!" The human placed the notes in my hand, tipped his hat, and turned to his mate. She scooped up the gem, fiddling with some kind of device. I could not tell what it was, but she put the gem deep inside it and closed it up.

"All set, Sam. This will work fine now. Are you ready to go?"

"Sure thing, Alice. I think Mr. and Mrs. Brady will be very happy with the anniversary gifts you've picked out. Good bye,

Achsmel!"

"Good bye, Achsmel!" The shorter female echoed her mate. Then she turned a dial on the device, and they vanished.

Things Look Different By Firelight

"You can't be serious, Professor Wagstaff. An invisible alien walking around, studying us? It sounds like the plot from an old science fiction periodical."

"Or the conspiracy theories of the Tinfoil Hat crowd. I know. But Captain Corcoran, my evidence leads to only this conclusion."

Corcoran leaned back in his chair and squinted at Wagstaff. A glance at the clock confirmed he had 15 minutes until lunch.

"Alright, Professor, let's have it. But be fast."

The professor placed his laptop on the captain's desk. He opened it and typed the password. Then he turned the screen to face the captain.

"This was taken last night. As you know, this base has the most advanced experimental security systems ever devised, including thermal, infrared, ultraviolet, magnetic, and air displacement sensors. What is unique is that we now can combine the readings into one video." Wagstaff hit the 'enter' key. "Watch."

Captain Corcoran reached out and adjusted the laptop screen to remove the glare from the fluorescent light above. He leaned in to study the scene. The front gate of the complex was laid out with the entrance road to the left and the complex to the right. The heads of two sentries could be seen in the gatehouse. Two more paced along the perimeter fence, night vision goggles scanning the area outside the base.

"Professor, I don't see…"

The captain gasped. A blurred form moved slowly to the fence, and then easily went up and over it. The guards' actions gave no indication they had seen anything.

"Have you interviewed these men, Wagstaff?"

"Yes, Captain. They swear they saw and heard nothing. One of them 'thinks' he smelled an odor, something like curry."

Captain Corcoran rubbed his chin and sat back.

"What else do you have?"

"Most of the data in that video was from the thermal and ultra violet sensors. Captain, whatever that thing was, its temperature was four degrees Celsius."

"Where did it go? I assume you also tracked it?"

"Look." Wagstaff pointed to the laptop again.

The screen now showed the captain the base's back up server room. Corcoran watched as the blur moved over to the terminal. The terminal's screen stayed dark, but flashing drive indicators throughout the racks of servers told the story.

"Smart. Reading the data from the back-ups. We don't have the same encryption there." Corcoran stood up.

"Professor, this is above my pay grade. We need to bring this to General Thatcher. Come on."

#

"Beginning transmission now."

The cave, while significantly more comfortable than the atmosphere outside, was still stifling.

"How are you doing, T'eree?"

"This entire planet is like a runaway sauna. How these bipeds evolved intelligence in this heat is a mystery to me. It will take an extensive effort to make it habitable. And it… it smells funny." T'eree Tur na'ar flinched his upper mandibles.

"Be thankful you're not an enviro-former, my friend. Transmission complete. If this truly is what you say, then the Council should make a decision soon."

"It will be good to see you again, Lor'aal." T'eree did not like to lie, but he desperately wanted out of this heat.

"These bipeds do everything backwards. They have their semi-growns breed and raise their young. How can semi-growns raise youngs? They have not the life experience."

"It is strange they do not have their matures raise their young. T'eree, does this mean you have completed the final stage of your evaluation?"

"No, Lor'aal. It will be a few cycles yet before I finish the final task. I will enjoy the sights of home all the more for it."

"It will be good to see you when that happens. Be safe, and Long Live The Empire. Signing off"

"Long live the empir…" T'eree stopped the mandatory salute when the signal was cut. He stood up and stretched his three legs, but had to bend at the thorax because of the low ceiling of the cave.

"My thirty seventh mission. Three more and I will be a full mature, able to retire with M'ree Hel't'on. Breeding the rest of my life away. Raising young ones." T'eree sighed.

"These bipeds are well armed. I hope the Council is sensible in their decision. If they choose landing troops over the bio-plague, many of our troops will die. It is not good to die before breeding."

#

"You are confident, Lor'aal? You are sure of the information T'eree has sent us?" The Great Council always spoke with one voice.

Lor'aal's triple steps echoed off the polished calcium crystal walls and floors of the Great Hall as he paced before the Great Council. He had prepared his presentations well, but this was the stage that would see him promoted or reduced.

"T'eree is our most experienced surveyor. He has never waivered from his mission. He has gathered the data from thirty six worlds. Worlds that are now important and thriving members of the Ma Urcs Brood H'eirs Empire. His recommendations have saved us many soldiers, soldiers now enhancing our forces by breeding prolifically.

"You have seen what he has sent us here. The data speaks for itself, Har'd'Eee.

"The system's star will keep the planet habitable for over a billion cycles. The system is far enough away from the Kest'onesKa Op'S to avoid an attack by them.

"The planet has abundant resources. The gravity is nearly perfect. The atmosphere is nearly perfect. It is unbearably hot, but adaptable. The planet has more than enough dihydrogen oxide to support ten billion workers. It has a large satellite that protects it from impacts.

"In short, Tes and Ovs of the Great Council, this planet is the most promising target we've seen this far out from the Galactic Core. We should prepare for the invasion pending T'eree's final report."

Lor'aal faced the center of the Great Council and bent his three knees. He spread his six arms and dropped his lower mandibles into his famous oratorical smile.

#

"This had better be damn good Corcoran. I'm missing a lunch date with my wife. I just may send you to absorb the fallout from that. Now, out with it!" General Thatcher was a big man, in a big position. His big voice fit right in.

"Sir, just watch the security tape. Go ahead, Professor."

Wagstaff set his laptop on the general's desk.

"Hold on, Wagstaff. Here, plug it in to the office sub base net so we can see it on the big screen."

"No, General. There is a bot on the base net that will remove any trace of what you will see. This is my last copy, assembled before the bot scrubbed the raw data feeds." Wagstaff turned the laptop's screen to face the general and hit the 'enter' key. "You can still see it here, watch."

"Someone, or something, has compromised our data. Who is it, Chinese? Israelis?"

"No sir. We don't believe it is…" Captain Corcoran flinched slightly, "Human. Sir."

Thatcher looked from Corcoran to Wagstaff, and back to Corcoran again.

"What?"

Captain Corcoran swallowed hard. Before he could answer, Professor Wagstaff chimed in.

"It's too cold. The alie… the intruder has a temperature of four degrees Celsius. No human would register that way. If it was a human wearing some kind of a thermal cloak, the heat would still have to go somewhere. This intruder is absorbing heat."

Thatcher sat back in his high backed chair, interlacing his fingers in his lap, and rolling his thumbs over each other. His eyes stared off into nowhere for several seconds, and then he sat forward with his hands on his desk.

"What data did it take?"

"Here?"

Both officers stared at Wagstaff with mouths agape.

"What the hell do you mean, 'here'?" Thatcher boomed.

"The bot we found in the net on this base is also on every military system used by the United States. And Canada. And Israel. And all of NATO. And Russia and China, too." Wagstaff swallowed heavily. "I, um... I checked."

The general and the captain glanced at each other, then back to the professor.

"Out with it. All of it." Thatcher rested his chin in his hands with his elbows on his desk.

"The hacki... eh, checking, or the..."

"JUST TELL US MAN!"

"Oh, a, okay then. We found the bot in our system after we lost several copies of the data and video. But we can't remove it. Damnedest thing. It's not hard to identify, really. Anyway, I had hacked into some of the other nets from time to time just to be sure there wasn't any of our data showing up there. To make sure they weren't able to hack us. You see, for some reason, no country ever has..."

"The bot, Professor!"

"Oh, yes. Well, I looked for it in Canada first. Their Niagara Falls research facility is studying infrared beam weapons just like we are. The bot was there.

"So, I looked at the Israeli research servers. It was there, too. I looked at NATO HQ servers, and into England, France, Germany. The bot was there.

"I looked at China. Russia. Bots. I even looked at Cuba, India, and Pakistan. Bots. And every place else I looked. Bots.

"The bots are in our electrical grid, communications, GPS. In short, they are everywhere. Wiping out all traces that our... intruder has been snooping around.

"This information would be crucial to an invading force, General."

"You're damned well right it would be. Hell, I'd want it if I were going to invade. The question is, what do we do about it?"

"We find it, General."

"But, doesn't it already have the information? What if it's already... left?"

"There is an astronomical amount of data for it to collect. Odds are that it's not done yet."

"Wait a minute. I thought you just said the bots were everywhere? Doesn't it follow then that the intruder has been everywhere the bots are?" Corcoran piped in.

"Not necessarily. The most efficient way to do this is to plant the bots first, then come in later and retrieve the data. If you planted the bots when you took the data, you could be discovered."

"How so?"

"Let's say you enter this base, and are about to plant the bot, when something funky happens, like a security drill or something, and you have to leave before the bot is planted. Bingo, you're found out!"

"So, how do we catch an invisible walking ice cube?"

#

T'eree tried not to move. The heat in the cave was barely tolerable. Outside, he could take it for only a few hours at a time. Those bases near the northern poles, now that was a nice working environment.

He would be here at least another tenth of a cycle. T'eree shot a glance at his rations. He would have to hunt. Soon. His mandibles quivered slightly at the memory of the local food.

#

"Now, children! Single file. Don't run, but move quickly."

"Yes, Mrs. Rittenhouse!" chimed the children's chorused response.

"Jackie, don't dawdle!"

"Yes, Ma'am."

As the group reached the doors, Margaret Rittenhouse opened the doors and held them.

"Come, Mickey, Mary Jane, Peggy. Jackie, keep up please!"

When the class had made it to their assigned station across the street from the school's main entrance, Mrs. Rittenhouse began counting heads.

"Everyone's here." She let out a breath she didn't remember taking in. "Class, good work. It took us 45 seconds to get here from our classroom." She always shivered a bit at this point in the fire drill.

What if it were real? Could I bring them out then?

"Ding-ding-ding"

"Alright class, line up! Good, Mickey. Peggy, Mary Jane! Stop chatting. Save it for lunch."

#

"Watch the target, Senator." Captain Spaulding yelled over the roar of the jet.

"That one?" Senator Hammer pointed straight ahead.

Yes, you moron. It's the only target!

"Yes, Senator."

As the two men watched, the five thousand pound block of ice instantly transformed from solid to liquid, the splash drowned out by the roar of the jet.

"I didn't see any beam!" Hammer turned to Captain Spaulding.

"You won't, Senator. The beam is infrared, beyond visible light."

"How long does it have to be on target to get that effect? I mean, so much ice instantly turning into water…"

"Actually, half of the ice sublimed directly into steam." Captain Spaulding stood and motioned the Senator to the waiting Humvee. "The beam you just witnessed fired for one tenth of a second."

"Damn! And how many shots does that F-22 carry?"

"The combat package will allow a total of twenty seconds of

firing time, Senator."

"Damn!"

"Just a short drive to the second target Senator." Captain Spaulding patiently held the door open.

#

"Professor, you're sure this equipment will find our visitor?"

"Still the skeptic, General?"

"Damn right, Captain. This stuff is too far above my physics pay grade."

"It will find him, General. I'm sure of it. I'm not sure it will fit in this vehicle though. Captain, if you please..." Wagstaff lifted one end of an electronic equipment rack. Corcoran bent and grabbed the other side.

"General, I wish you'd reconsider, Sir. This could be dangerous. I assume he's armed."

"Captain Corcoran, being a general has its drawbacks and its perks." Thatcher helped slide the rack into place inside the Humvee. "One of those perks is going on a mission to catch an alien when regs suggest I shouldn't. Besides, we're just spotlighting him. The troops will move in to make the capture. And, we're armed too. It is getting crowded in here, Professor."

"Give me a few minutes to get it all hooked up. I'm using a GPS interface, so you just follow the route to find him."

"Why are you two calling it 'he' and 'him'? We don't know if it even has sex differentiation."

"General, you're too PC. It's just a matter of expedience. Would you feel better if we referred to the alien as 'her'?"

"How about 'it', professor?"

"Suggests an inanimate object. Not a good idea."

"We do need a 'code name'. We could call it duck."

"Why a duck?"

General Thatcher shrugged.

"Hey, you're the scientist."

#

It was more tolerable to hunt at night, but T'eree was hungry now. He should have eaten some of his rations and hunted at darkness, but there was more data to collect. And, he was also curious.

Soon he would send his final report and leave this place. But first he needed to know about these bipeds.

Would they even fight? The empire was always happy to find new slaves. Would they be a pestilence, fighting to the bitter end? The answer would mean the difference between a bio-attack that killed all the bipeds, but left the other life in place, or an invasion of soldiers taking slaves.

T'eree hit the med dispenser on his harness. The needle shot into his fourth armpit, delivering the measured dose of the drug that helped him deal with this oppressive heat.

A quick check of his electronics package showed his screen was still up. These bipeds were only aware of a small portion of the light spectrum, so it was easy to move about undetected.

At the entrance to the cave, T'eree scanned his surroundings. Food, off to his right, just a few strides away.

T'eree took off at a gallop. The food never saw him. He stopped next to it, reached underneath and opened it up with his fifth arm. The attack was swift enough that the food never made a sound. It fell, the insides spilling out. Just move this, and there it is!

T'eree scanned his surroundings. It wouldn't do to have a biped see this food rise up and disappear.

Satisfied of his seclusion, T'eree ate.

#

Major Otis Driftwood banked his F-22 lazily to his left. This bird could virtually fly itself, but right now Driftwood was enjoying a few banks to kill the time. His next firing pass was scheduled for two minutes from now, giving him some time to enjoy the scenery.

"I wonder what happens when this thing is used in combat?" he said outloud. "If the beam hits the canopy, the pilot gets cooked. Fuel, ammo, the plane blows up. Structure, it melts away and the plane's unflyable. And all I have to do is look at a target within range and blink."

Major Driftwood banked the F-22 to his left, scanning the ground around him.

"Huh! Must be some wolves around here, maybe a mountain

lion? Whatever it was, it sure laid that cow open."

#

T'eree watched the machine fly overhead. A reasonable piece of technology, but limited to the thicker parts of the atmosphere. His sensors told him the machine couldn't detect him, so he ignored it.

Feeling calmer now that he'd eaten, T'eree moved towards the biped settlement nearby. His three legged gallop moved him quickly over the landscape. There was a lot of food here.

He came upon a large structure. There were many bipeds inside, but most were small. They seemed to be clustered in small groups with one or two larger bipeds, evenly distributed throughout the structure.

A training center!

"This is a perfect place to learn the mettle of these creatures."

#

"This way, Captain. To the right." Wagstaff directed, turning dials on his equipment. "It *was* here. Not long ago."

"Captain! Stop! Look, in the field!" General Thatcher was out the Humvee's door almost before it stopped. Captain Corcoran sprinted to catch up to the old man. *Not a good career move, having a General killed under your watch,* he thought.

The two officers stopped at the edge of the field, soon joined by the professor. The three stared at the gory mess in front of them.

"It's been cut open."

"Gee, how'd you figure that out, Professor?" Corcoran shook his head and moved closer.

"Heart. Lungs, all the stomachs, intestines, kidneys... The liver's not here."

"Livers are packed with nutrients. It fed here. We should keep moving."

"Yeah." Thatcher glanced up at the circling jet.

"Shit!"

"General?" Corcoran froze.

"The IR beam demonstration for Senator Hammer." Thatcher pointed at the F-22 circling towards the town. "I was supposed to be there. I just hope Spaulding doesn't make a SNAFU of it!"

"Oh, my God! What was that?"

"C'mon!"

#

"Hey, that looks like General Thatcher," Major Driftwood watched the three men enter the Humvee near the dead cow. "I wonder why he's not ushering the Senator around the demo. Shit!"

Driftwood pulled back hard on the stick. He'd been in combat mode, which meant most of the flight safety alarms had been muted. Now his collision alert was blaring. When he looked to the nose of the F-22 Raptor, the trees ahead of him were way too close.

Otis hit the afterburners to keep the huge fighter from stalling. The roar from the torrent of raw fuel pouring into the jet's twin exhaust was deafening.

Stall warning alarms, vital in combat, told Driftwood that his plane would soon become a brick, as the airflow over his wings was almost too slow to provide lift. The fighter shuddered under the stress of the pull up and the afterburners.

The geese had been feeding, concentrating on the scattered corn kernels and bugs in the field. It wasn't a huge flock, only twenty-two birds.

The roar of afterburners burst over the tree line at the far end of the field. The geese reacted instinctively.

They took flight.

Major Otis Driftwood fought to hold his ship in the air. The first goose hit the left wing, shattering the aerodynamics of that lifting surface. The next hit the center of his canopy, shattering it. Shards of jagged plastic hit him, one piece lodging in his neck. Three more geese hit the Raptor, shredding the left engine and crumpling the control surfaces.

The last goose went through the fighter's shattered canopy and crushed Major Driftwood's throat.

#

T'eree stood in the rear of the classroom. He'd been there long enough to sense the personalities of the young bipeds. So curious! The way their eyes lit up when understanding came. So much like the young on his homeworld. His mind drifted, thinking of M'ree Hel't'on, dreaming of breeding his own young ones with her... their own young ones...

The deafening roar jerked him out of his dream. The room had collapsed around him, a few of the young bipeds, and the larger one. Dust, smoke... Fire!

That flying machine must have found him and attacked. *No, that made no sense. The bipeds would not have attacked him this close to their young ones! They could not be that barbaric!*

His right leg hurt, and two of his arms refused to move. The pain was intense. He could see the larger biped gathering the young ones, trying to open the door in vain.

What was their word for it... *crying.*

He saw the flames, felt the heat. T'eree trembled.

THE TERROR!

T'eree had to fight his instincts to blindly flee. He had to use reason. But the flames! The flames stalked him!

The flying machine must have malfunctioned and crashed into this structure.

Already the heat tortured him. The flames were coming!

His med unit jabbed a needle into him. His pain eased a little and his mind cleared a bit.

The fire came closer. His leg was broken. The heat was injuring him severely, bubbling his flesh even though the meds muted the pain.

Worse was the fear, the terror that fire held for him.

If I go now, I may be able to get out through this rubble behind me. The young ones...

The panic among the bipeds was obvious. T'eree thought of his own young trapped like this, watching the flames come closer.

They looked at him, and T'eree knew they could see him. One moved close to him and reached out towards his injured arm.

The young biped's touch was very warm, but tender. It reminded T'eree of his broodmate's young. He looked at the approaching flames again, fought through the panic, and tried to stand up.

#

"Good God no. The school!" General Thatcher flew out of the Humvee and to the steps of the burning building, followed closely by Captain Corcoran and Professor Wagstaff.

"I think all of the kids are out," a dazed looking man in a dusty suit and tie spoke to the uniforms in front of him, "except for Mrs. Rittenhouse's class."

"Here! We. We're over here!" Margaret Rittenhouse called from the side of the building. "All the children, they're here. It, it pulled us..." The battered teacher fainted.

#

"His life sign transmissions have ceased. T'eree is dead. We cannot approve an invasion to a planet that claimed the Great

T'eree.

"Lor'aal, you will find another target. Until then, we continue the lowered breeding quotas.

"The Great Council will adjourn until next cycle."

#

"Professor! General! Here!" Captain Corcoran crouched down next to the charred remains.

"My! Will you look at that!"

"Three legs. Six arms. Given the body temperature we had seen earlier, the heat must have been torture for that thing."

"Four trips, she said it made. Back into the flames. Until they were all out. Then once more. It got this far, dragging Driftwood's body until the flames caught up with them."

What Is So Precious

What is it, so precious
that we strive so hard for?

What is it, so precious
that pains us so terribly?

What is it, so precious
that drives us up the unscalable?

What is it, so precious
that tests our souls incessantly?

What is it, so precious
that we cling to so tenaciously?

What is it, so precious?

It is

us.

fortiterpublishing.com

Who, Me?

Some call me a hero. I dunno 'bout dat. I'll tell ya what happened, den *you* decides.

So, I'm in Central Park, see, and I gotsta take a leak, ya know? So I use one of dem fancy outhouse-type rigs da city puts 'round. When I comes out, well, everting happened den. Real quick-like. Go figger.

I comes out and here was dis big, *ting*. All shiny grey an' metal-like, but shimmerin'. Like da air over the street in July, ya know? Enee-way, I sees dis ramp on da right side of dis ting. Big 'nuff for a coupla busses side-by-side. I just stares at it fer a while, takin' it all in, ya know? Den deese big tings come down da ramp, see, like da Michelin Man er somethin'. But 'bout ten feet tall, and witt three legs! Three legs! I ain't never seen *dat* before. Not nowhere.

Anyway, six of deese brutes come down dat ramp, and starts off aways from me, towards Columbus Coircle, carryin' deese big Bazooka-like tings, cabled into a big hump on dere backs, like flamethrowers in olden war movies. Septin' this wasn't no movie.

Well, dey's a trottin' down da ramp, an' one of 'em drops dis ting. It jus' falls offa him! Like, day all had deese tings, like soffballs, but a little bigger, hangin' offa der belts, an' one of 'em

38

jus falls off!

So, deese tings are gone now, an dis soffball-like ting is dere, so I goes and picks it up. Now, I dunno why, but somethin' told me to act real careful-like, so dat's what I was doin'. Anyhow, I picks up dis ting, and it is HEAVY! It musta been like ten, fifteen pounds. So, I'm lookin' ats it, and I sees a little ring, and a bunch of squiggles on it, like writin', but no letters like I never seen. Well, justabout den I hears sometin, and I looks where dem tings went to, an' one of 'em's comin' back!

So, I figgers real quick-like, that he's afta da ting he dropped dat I'm a-holdin'! So, I'm lookin' ta scram, ya know? Like, get outta Dodge in a hurry. So I trows dis ting dat dis big fella's comin' back fer, but it won't go. I look, an' da ring's caught on my shoit. So, I'm like panickin' now, and I pulls real hard, and da ring comes right off!

Well, I'm still hurryin' like, so I tosses da ball as far away as I can. Funny, as heavy as it was, it wents real far whens I tossed it. I tinks it went up da ramp. So, den I slips back inside da John. Hey, it was da bestest hidin' spot around!

Anyway, I looks out troo da door, an' sees da guy, er, whatever it was, lookin' around on da ground, den he looks up, den da fire comes down da ramp and fries 'im. Like, nuttin' left at all. Den I sees da rest of dem tings comin' back, in a real hurry-like. Deere lookin' around, and two of 'em go up da ramp. Inna coupla minutes dey comes out, an' deys all gathers in a tight li'l group. Den, dey each hits sumtin on deere chests, and POOF! Dey all explodes in a big flash!

Well, I stays in dat John, and in a bit, cops show up. Lots o' cops! Den some Army-types. After a few, I comes out an 'ventuly tells 'em da story I just tol' you. I shows 'em da ring, it's still caught on me shoit. One of 'em, a bossy-type, a Major, I tinks, tells me I'm a hero, dat I saveded us from invasion.

I dunno 'bout dat. Hero. Ha!

Who, me?

Yeah. Right.

Looking for Master

I didn't mean to run away! Honest! Sometimes I just can't help myself.

Master had told me we were going home. To Earth. The place Master was born. Earth is the best place for my kind, Master said.

But, the sights! The sounds! The smells! Master said it was a Port, where we would get on a thing and then we would be at Earth. A Port is a very scary place. All those people, moving very quickly, noises, smells; it all frightened and excited me.

Part of me wanted to go explore everything. Part of me wanted to cower and hide in a safe place. I huddled as close to Master as I could.

Master's soothing words helped some. Until that big bang.

I don't know what made the loud bang. Such things are often beyond me; so many things in the Master's world are. I just know the loud bang made me panic just as Master turned away. I was very frightened, so pushed Master away and I ran.

Terrified, I ran past the people, a lot of people. More people than I had ever seen in one place before. It was hard weaving around them at a full run, but I am very good at such things. And I was very frightened.

I heard Master call after me. Master's voice was very far away, and soon was gone. I could not see Master, or smell

Master. I do not remember another time when that was so. It frightened me even more, so I ran and ran.

I finally came upon a place to hide, so I slid in and crouched down behind some bags. They were like the ones Master carried, but they were a different skin, a different color, and they smelled very different. But they hid me.

I shivered in fear. I panted with exhaustion and heat. Where was Master? When I had run away in fear before, Master came looking. Master was always very kind to me after I was found. Master? Where are you? I tried to call Master, but my voice only squeaked a little.

We were rushing to catch a something that would take us home. I am good at catching things. I catch things for Master all the time. We were rushing because we were late, and the thing was going to leave without us if we didn't run fast. Well, Master does not run fast, like me.

But I am sure now that Master has gone to Earth. A half-day after I ran, the Port quieted down, well past twilight hunting time. I went looking for Master. I found some food; that was easy, as food was everywhere in the Port.

I looked all over the Port. It was very big, like Master's house, only much bigger. And I could not get out of the Port, not like Master's house, where I had my own door to go in and out as I pleased.

I found a place to nap, and slept some. Then, after dawn

hunting time, the Port got very noisy and busy again. This time, it did not frighten me quite so much, but I still hid. And I watched, and listened.

I heard some people talk about Earth; the place the Master was taking me before I ran away. Most of Master's talking is lost to me, but some I can understand. I watched, and followed them. They stopped and waited near a door, with a lot of other people. Master was not with them.

I hid among their things, and soon noticed a lot of new people coming through the door. Many of them came through, and they all smelled, well, different. I wonder if this must be what Earth smells like? Then no new ones came. The new people all moved away, like they didn't want to be in the Port.

After a short time, the people waiting started moving through the door. I thought I should go, as I missed Master very much. So I snuck through the door among the people, and into a small room that reminded me of Master's car, but much bigger. Master sometimes took me for rides in the car, but I really did not like that very much. It made me dizzy.

I moved into the big car, and I smelled it! Master had been here! I am very good at smelling.

I found a place to hide, and waited. Maybe Master would come back, and take me home. I missed Master very much.

The people all stopped moving around, and the big car started to shake, and made very loud noises. I was frightened, so

I crouched down in my hiding place and I shivered in fear. The scent of Master helped, a little.

The big car began moving, and that made me dizzy, just like Master's car, but worse. Then the moving stopped, and I felt better. The noise was still loud, though. I was still scared.

The worst was when the big car blinked. It went dark-bright-dark very fast. I felt really dizzy then, like I was falling in every direction. The whole car seemed to blur. Some things floated in air. The people looked stretched. I was very frightened. Then it went dark-bright-dark very fast again, and everything looked normal. I still felt like I would throw up, though.

The big car got noisier for a time, and moved more. Then it stopped and got quiet. I heard someone say "Earth", and all the people left the big car.

I followed them out, and I could smell that Master had been here, so I followed that scent. I was in a different Port!

I followed the scent of Master. Sometimes it was on the floor, some times in the air-that was harder. By staying in the middle of a lot of people, I was able to leave the Port. But my feet got stepped on a few times.

Outside was noisy, much more noisy than outside Master's house. It was hard to smell Master, but I kept following the scent. I had to stop to hunt three times, since Master was not with me to give me food. I think I like hunting for my own food better.

Once I had caught some food, and some people saw me

carrying it off so I could eat in private. I don't share food. One of the people made the loud, angry noise that Master makes sometimes. I don't like that noise.

I followed Master's scent for a long time. The outdoors soon became quieter.

Then, just after morning hunting time, I came upon a place that looked a lot like Master's house, but different. It smelled like Master, a lot! I just had to find Master now, I had found Master's Earth house.

I went up to the door, on the quiet side of the house, and looked in. I couldn't see much, but then, I saw Master's Master!

Master's Master opened the door, and made all kinds of happy sounds, hugging me. Master's Master brought me up high in the house. I smelled Master! Not just Master's scent, but MASTER!

I ran again. Right into a room, and there was Master!

I jumped up into Master's lap. I laid down in her lap, curled-up, and began purring. It seemed like the right thing to do.

One Is A Lonely Number

It had been a long hike. He'd climbed mountains, waded across streams, hacked through forests, jungles really. Two weeks it had taken to get here.

He hoped it was worth the trip.

Oh, he'd gained some good information along the way. Not that he'd had any choice.

He felt like he weighed five hundred pounds. He could breathe the thin air here, drink the water, and eat some of the fruit.

And he knew something was stalking him.

But he was here now!

He could get supplies, maybe call for help.

The area was heavily vegetated. Vines climbed up huge trees, bushes and shrubs crowded beneath.

He hacked through a wall of green for the hundredth time.

There it was!

He took in a big breath at the sight. Hope buoyed his spirits.

Practicality brought him to ground.

The area around it was burned, but already thin green shoots rose up. The homing beacon gave out three days ago. A few more weeks and he would never have found it.

A quick glance behind him, then he ran.

The fifty yard sprint left him gasping at the door. He punched in the code.

Nothing happened.

He glanced behind him again. Still clear…

He ripped the emergency panel off and pulled the handle. Fifty pumps to open the door.

Leaves rustled behind him.

The handle came off in his hand.

He looked along the charred metal. There, the handholds!

He scrambled up, moving only a few feet off of the ground before exhaustion froze him.

It would be enough.

As long as it couldn't climb the handholds.

He tried to think. Where was he? Where was the other lock? Would it open?

He had to try.

The ashes and shoots rustled below. It was circling, waiting.

A few minutes gave him his breath back. He noticed the metal, scraped and scoured. To his left it was torn, peeled back. Like a banana he thought. He could go through there, but the metal would be dangerously twisted.

He pulled himself up, almost on the top. The metal seemed to end just beyond the next handhold.

He spent a few minutes panting in the thin air.

He reached out and pulled himself forward.

Gone!

He glanced at the ground behind him. The movements of the plant stalks showed the thing's movements.

Carefully he slid over the edge. The three layers of metal were bent into themselves, keeping any sharp edges from his path. He swung over the side and let go.

It wasn't a long fall, only about five meters. But he hit hard.

The crack sounded in his ears well before the pain told him the rib was broken.

He managed to crawl to the hatch. The code he entered did nothing.

Of course! No power.

This hatch opened when he pumped the handle.

It only took him an hour.

It would be almost around to the open side by now.

He could barely breathe. The pain, the thin air. He must be bleeding inside.

He opened the last of his oxygen supply. It helped some. He managed to raise a foot and push the hatch closed before he passed out.

The pain in his head woke him.

Low oxygen.

He pulled the spent oxygen mask off and threw it aside.

His rib screamed.

Perfect darkness. No breaches here.

He hit his light.

The communications gear, next to him.

He hit the controls.

Lights!

"May-day! May-day! May-day! Crashed…" The coughs battered him. "Alpha Cigna Epsilon Eight. Emergency…"

Sparks flew from the comm gear.

Then it went dark.

He could hear the thing outside the hatch, slithering back and forth.

Everything faded into blackness…

The blaring alarms woke him. His eyes complained about the bright lights.

Bright lights!

"Major hull breach! Atmosphere venting! Abandon ship! Major hull breach! Atmosphere venting! Abandon ship!" the ship's computer screamed at him.

He dove into the escape pod.

The acceleration nearly made him black out. When it stopped, he hit the emergency beacon and opened the computer files on the nearest planet.

Thin air, heavy gravity, vegetation. Unknown animal life.

He knew what was there.

And that it was waiting for him…

Silly Question

The village knight was busy sharpening his spear when his daughter tugged on his kilt.

"Daddy, what do dragons eat?" the seven-year-old red headed girl asked.

"Well, lass," the knight replied without looking up, "Dragons eat people."

"Oh. OK. Thank you, Daddy" she replied before turning away and skipping on down the lane.

After eating the knight, the dragon skipped along behind her.

The Agony Of Defeat

The whistle blew, ending the chaos. I looked up at the clock, trying to avoid the score emblazoned there. Three, two, one. Suddenly I felt tired, old, sore. I let out a deep breath I didn't remember taking in.

47 to 44. Losing was not good. My eyes followed the team, bloodied and bruised, slogging off the field. Three games in a row. One more and there will be a new Captain for sure. Maybe even today.

I followed them into the dressing room. It didn't take long for the small space to fill with the stench of sweat, blood, and dirt. The team mulled about, letting the loss drip off them with their sweat. Down, defeated, beaten.

Dead.

"Good effort, men. But we need more. We have the tools to win the next game. We will hone them in two days. Practice Wednesday at 9:00AM sharp."

My voice was as pitiful, but sounded better than I had thought it would. I limped stiffly to my cubicle and glanced at the whirlpool. The line was long.

Damn.

I sat on the bench. After a time of studying my cleats, I pulled the jersey and shoulder pads over my head as a unit. The cold air hit my drenched tee shirt as the jersey steamed at my feet. A strong odor like garlic and vanilla told me not to look up. The bench moved, so I turned to look at the feet of whoever sat next to me.

"Aille m'scrundlat, hgsta frengol whet-wet. Tellna d'rec mortin waster fin."

"Do you want to remove me now, Master?"

"Norint. Aille m'scrundlat grelaelt. Hastre..."

"Thank you, Master." All emotion drained from me. "Which ones?"

"Anderson, McCauliffe, aaehr... Simon."

Only three. The Skorlt who owned us got off with a light sentence. That meant we did, too.

"Yes, Master. When will the replacements arrive?"

"Scralpt! Wesstellam melt rik jaustein!"

"Sorry, Master."

The Skorlt left. I reached into my cubby and pulled out the knife and the mat. I placed the mat on the floor.

"Anderson! McCauliffe! Simon!"

The three nervously came forward. I pointed to the mat with the knife. Simon glanced at the Skorlt guards by the door, then joined the other two in assuming the position. Hands and knees on the mat, head bent forward, forehead touching the mat.

The rest of the team kept their backs to us. I was thankful for that.

Simon was shaking, so I went to him first. I placed the tip of the knife on the back of his neck where it joined his head, angled towards the top of it.

They tell me you don't feel a thing this way.

Only the dead slaves really know.

Boxed In

"Really, it was all rather un-exciting. Are you sure you want to hear it?" The reporter had said she wanted an exclusive interview before I gave my speech. Since my entire campaign was based on the 'average guy vs. the political-industrial complex', I figured I had to grant it. Besides, what did I have to worry about? The election was ten days away, and I had 65% of the vote in the polls.

She was short, dark brown hair, sort of frumpy-looking. She had on a knit ski-cap, glasses, and a dark sweater over jeans and sneakers. Smokey didn't like her; that should have tipped me off. The big Siamese liked everyone, even those taken aback by his seven toes and twenty-five pound heft.

"No, please, tell me about your life before your work for General Origenetics Developments. Most people have an idea of your life since you began working there, but none of us know anything about what you did before that."

She reached into her large bag, and took out a pad and pencil. Really, no computer, recorder, or tablet, but a pad and paper! That should have been clue number two.

"OK, but all the juicy parts my opponent has already told you about. Along with several that never happened. Um, that was a joke, you're supposed to pretend to laugh now." *Good grief, what brand of mind-numbed robot have they sent me?*

She just stared at me over the top of her glasses. Even her eyes were unattractive. I've never seen nor heard of that, her eyes were definitely unattractive.

"Well, how far back shall I go?" *Will she fall for this? Has she heard of Chico Marx?*

"Oh, right to the beginning."

"Well," *hook, line, and sinker, too easy,* "I started out as a child...."

OK, no more jokes. She makes HAL 9000 look like Groucho!

"I grew up, went to school. I did OK. Actually, I had the highest SATs my senior year. I played football, ran track. Longed after girls, but was too shy to talk to them. Pretty average. Pretty boring.

"I went to college, goofed off, got on academic probation, and didn't go back. I worked. I met a girl I could talk too, convinced her to marry me. We had a couple of kids, I went back to college. Got my RRT, worked in a hospital, got fed up with the idiots in charge of it, and quit. My wife took the kids and left. So I went looking for work, and found General Origenetics Developments. It helped that the founder is an old school buddy. How's that?"

"Sort of boring. Is that it?"

I told you that before! HRUMPF!!!

"Yeah. That's it. Well, except for the depression diagnosis. And, once my OSA was diagnosed and treated, that went away."

"What about your porn history?"

"I used to go into a porn shop when I was young. So did every other male between thirteen and seventy those days. It was a way to deal with being disappointed in myself. That stopped with the OSA treatment, and other changes in my life."

"You found Jesus?"

"I would have had to have been looking for him to 'find' him. No, I just realized I was punishing myself. So I had a long talk about it. God was listening, and sort of butted in. I let him into the conversation."

"So, God 'eavesdropped' on you? Yet you run against the government doing just that. Are you saying it's OK for God to help some people, but not the government? Statistics have shown that the First Intervention Safety Technology programs have stopped thousands of suicides and mass murders..."

"Are you saying that the government acts as God? Really? And, who puts out the statistics you cite?"

"Well, the FIST program does."

"And, exactly how does this FIST grow? By showing how great it is? By releasing whatever numbers it wants to as 'statistics' that justify it's own expansion? The only people the FIST programs serve are their own bureaucrats! The government has no business spying on every phone call, vid call, text, and email that every person makes."

"It has been said that you have managed to communicate without the government or your employer being aware of it.

How did you do that?"

"Simple. And well known; I used pen and paper. Just like you are now."

"Oh. Tell me how your career went at General Origenetics Developments."

"That too is public knowledge. Why re-hash it?"

"Well, just so we get the story straight…"

"Excuse me one second. Yes, Charles? Really? Amazing. No, no, don't re-schedule anything. I'll take care of it. Thank you, Charles. Now, Miss…I didn't catch your name? May I pour you a drink? Iced tea, diet cola, root beer, apple cider?" I poured myself an apple cider.

"No, thank you. My name is Sylvia. Sylvia Anderson. Now, what about…"

"What about your press credentials? They don't compute." I turned and faced her. It would come soon.

"Why, whatever do you mean?"

"What news agency do you report to?"

"I report to AP."

"Interesting. AP has no female reporters in this state right now. Are you wearing a wig?"

"No, I, um…"

"What is your real name? Sylvia Anderson the reporter died two years ago."

"What are you accusing me of?"

"Hm. Not sure, yet. What exactly have you done? You do realize that there is an ultra high frequency beacon in this room that makes any recording you're making, or anything you're broadcasting useless, don't you?" *Where are you from? A political party? General Origenetics Developments? FBI?*

"I think the question becomes what threat you pose, Mr. Dalton. You have shut down a company providing replacement organs at reasonable prices. The public's access to organ transplants had been ..."

"Wait, reduced what, exactly? Of course it's been reduced! Government health insurance pays so little for transplants the average person can't afford one! The only 'access' that General Origenetics provided was to the super rich! The organs were not grown in pristine isolation, as we were told; they were grown as integral parts of young adult humans who were 'matured' from genetically modified 'test-tube' fetuses! And the tiny quota of low priced organs supplied to government hospitals aren't even *from humans*! So, I ask you again, what is your name and who do you report to?"

She tried to fire her gun then. It was really pretty lame, since I saw it before I gave my little rant. So did Smokey; he was on her back, pumping his hind legs until those fourteen claws had reached her skin. She was close enough for me to slap the patch on her neck. The anesthetic was fast acting and harmless. The patch would keep her groggy for about four hours. My other hand reached for her gun. I grabbed it and pointed it down and away from me. It went off, and that's when I realized my third finger was over the barrel.

Oh, I went out anyway and gave the speech. I even brought her out and told the audience what had happened, then asked the State Police to arrest her. I showed the crowd the bandage on my finger, er, stump. That was really hurting by then. I even showed the vid from my security camera. Then I lead a prayer for her. The live audience went nuts. I heard the television audience did too. Poll numbers two days later showed me with 88% of the vote. And climbing.

I'm assuming that someone out there does not like that.

I'll bet they don't.

Not one bit.

Be Careful What You Wish For...

He jumped up, face all red, eyes bulging; "That was a CHARGE! Damn refs! Fixing the game AGAIN!"

"Jim, calm down! You'll have a stroke or something!"

"Did you see that? They call it one way on one end of the court, then change the rules on the other end! These refs STINK!" Jim sat back down, still fuming as he always did when watching his team.

"There they go AGAIN!" Jim yelled as he threw the pillow down. "Bastards! They don't have a chance with refs like that! Fixed! By the bookies!"

"I'm going up to Dad's house 'till the game's over", Cindy said. She just hated the noise, the anger Jim showed when he got like this.

"OK hon. I'm sorry." Jim said meekly.

Soon, with Cindy gone and the house to himself, Jim was even louder, less constrained.

"GOD_DAMMIT!!! They're fixing it! What I wouldn't give to get inside their heads! Make them be honest. They...the...eh....agh....."

Cindy found him when she came home after the game, in the middle of the living room floor, unresponsive. The ambulance took him away shortly after.

Jim woke up all alone. He didn't know where he was, but he did remember the game. He thought about the refs, and as soon as he pictured one, he *WAS* inside his head!

It was all so simple, like placing silverware in a place setting. Jim could see it all: the gambler threats and bribes, the ref's plan to fix the score. Changing it was as simple as moving a knife and fork: take this from here, set it down over there, and PRESTO! Honest ref!

But it couldn't stop there, for Jim had seen the gambler's threats; the ref's family was at risk. So Jim thought of the gambler, and there was the table, all laid out for him! Pick this up, set it down over here....and.....the gambler is an honest man!

It took some time. There were a lot of referees, and even more gamblers. But soon, Jim had everything on the level, all on the up-n-up. Jim smiled, and drifted off to sleep.

"I'm sorry, Mrs Jones, but Jim is gone. Frankly, I can't believe he lasted these six months."

"Thank you, doctor, for everything. The sad part is, since Jim went into that coma, every game he would have watched was, well, different. It's like it was all made right....."

His First Dance

"Stupid, stupid, STUPID!" He kicked at the snow as he walked. "My first dance ever, and I get to slow-dance with Madeline Ross! I ask her to go steady. Sally tells me she's gunna say "yes." and I make a dumb remark. STUPID! Now she won't talk to me AT ALL."

He stuffed his hands into the pockets of his unzipped jacket. His head was cold, because he couldn't find his hat, and he was too upset to pull his hood up. He had another half mile to walk before he got home. Every few minutes a police car sped past; otherwise, he had only the glow from an occasional streetlight to keep him company. The trees cast spooky shadows that stretched far in front of him.

"My parents are gunna be mad, too. I'll probably get grounded for like a thousand years. Darn Johnny Haskell."

He kicked at the snow again.

"I shouldn'ta done it. Darn it all, I shouldn'ta done it! Dad gave it to me for emergencies, and told me to be careful with it. Then Johnny Haskell went and kissed her! "

He stopped, turned around and looked back the way he came, hoping. After a moment he turned back and started walking.

"I shouldn'ta done it! Darnitall!" He stopped again, thinking.

"Maybe it won't be so bad. Maybe Dad'll give me a break.

They're only humans, after all."

He turned and looked back again.

"Nah, I'm screwed. Dad said we have to learn from them. This'll screw up everything! DARNITALL!"

The mushroom cloud was still growing. He looked down, turned around and started walking home again.

"Yup. Grounded. A thousand years. At least. And probably on Alpha Proxima, too! I HATE that stupid boring old planet."

He kicked at the snow once again as he walked.

A Dark Dream's Hell

The idea came to me in a dream.

A dozen grackles chased me through the graveyard. Big, noisy, oily-dark things. They relentlessly flew after me. As fast as I ran, still they were upon me. I tried to run, to hide, but I couldn't escape. In desperation, I tried to imagine what they were seeing.

Quite a simple idea, really. Yet, rather than seeing a means of escaping my tormentors, I found myself as one of them, looking down at the clumsy man trying to run away from me.

I awoke at that instant. The night air chilled me to the core, aided by the sweat-drenched bedclothes. But I had the idea!

A splash of water to my clammy face and I flew down the stairs. Mrs. Higgins awoke at my clamor, asking why I was up at this ungodly hour. I directed her to bring some strong coffee to my laboratory straight away.

I set to work immediately, building the device for the engram transfer. How I knew what to do, I cannot say. I can only say that the device was ready by noon.

I needed subjects for a trial.

Despite Mrs. Higgins's diligent service with the coffee, I was exhausted from my efforts. I sat at the window, the mid day sun warming me considerably. I reached up, opened the portal, and a grackle flew in to land upon my machine. The creature seemed very comfortable there, his bottomless eyes scanning the device before coming to stare relentlessly at me. A sudden noise from outside the window broke my stupor. A dozen more of the iridescent birds screamed and clamored while flying as arrows right for me!

I jumped with a start, a scream escaping past my lips. I backed away, yet on they came, feathers swirling, beaks squawking, talons reaching, reaching, reaching...

I stumbled over the table and lost my balance. My head hit something, and blackness flooded the world.

I awoke soon enough. Something was pulling at my head. Perhaps I had bled? I turned and spied the mirror then.

I had fallen into my device, the connections somehow about my head. The shock must have jarred the first bird into the machine as well, for he was likewise connected. A glance at the controls completed my horror as the grackles lit upon them, pecking at them, setting my accursed machine into motion.

Since then, I have seen my body rise and run away. I have seen Mrs. Higgins scream at this same sight. Now I stand on the sill of my own laboratory window.

I have decided upon a course of action. I only need find another to build my machine, and plant the idea some how. Then will I find escape from this feathered prison, either through death, or through a life lived as some other man.

Now, if I can only find some one capable, and plant the dream...

One Little Mistake

They all blame me. It's not fair!

Any one of them could have prevented it, they were the adults, they had the responsibility, after all. But they all blame me. The Wonder Boy.

Wonder Boy. Hah! All my life they've called me that. All fourteen years of it. I liked it when I was seven. By the time I was eight, I cringed whenever I heard it. Hey, grad school astrophysics is tough enough on an eight year old without *that* kind of pressure!

It all began with my thesis on neutron-plasma drives for space ships. Basically, you crush a hydrogen atom until the proton and electron combine. This releases a huge amount of energy, which turns the resulting neutron into super-heated plasma that rushes out of the reaction chamber at around 99% of the speed of light. It gives you a huge amount of thrust from a tiny amount of fuel. Use a liter per minute of hydrogen, and you get enough thrust to go from Earth to Mars in like two days, Jupiter in four and a half.

So, when I defend my thesis, there is a guy in a grey suit there I don't know. Like, talk about nervous! After my defense, this guy introduces himself as Jim Walters, head of NASA. He wanted me to help NASA build the engine!

Well, my dad and the lawyers had all the patent stuff dealt with, and I was tired of school, so I went to build the engine and help them design a ship to use it.

We built a few small test designs that worked just like I said they would, after I had brought all those old engineers up to speed. Jeeze, thirty, forty years old and still making simple mistakes! Yeah, these are the morons who blame me.

After three years of small scale testing, we began working on the full-scale engine. We couldn't fire it up on Earth; the exhaust would screw up the weather, so NASA decided to put it on the moon. Not my decision, but they still blame me.

It took a year to get all the stuff up there we needed; housing, power, computers, all that kind of stuff. Then it took another year to get all the parts of the engine to the moon, and the water to make the hydrogen from. That gave me free time. I spent most of it with Mr. Walters' daughter, Jane. She's fifteen, and pretty cute, and not too dumb. At some point last summer, I promised her the moon. As I said, she's pretty cute.

Then we fired up the engine.

The exhaust made a wonderful show when seen from Earth. All bright blue and orange, stretching across half the sky. You could even see it in the daytime. None of them thought a thing about it then. Now they all blame me.

We had planned to let the engine run for sixty days straight, to test reliability for flights to other stars. Then we would shut it down, wait a month, and restart it, just like on a real mission.

It was after twenty days that I noticed it. We were sitting on Mr. Walters' porch, Jane and I, talking, and looking at the moon. She said it looked so big, and reached out and held my hand. I was real nervous, but then it hit me; the moon DID look big! Way, way too big. And, it was moving across the sky way too fast!

It took me two whole hours to make them understand and shut the engine down. It was too late by then. That's when they started blaming *me*.

The engine had been built on the edge of the moon as you see it from Earth, so we could observe the exhaust better. The moon orbits the Earth with that side as the leading edge. My engine acted as a giant retro rocket for the moon.

I figured in my head that we had about six months before the moon crashed into the Earth. The computers confirmed I was right about that. Not that it matters. Not nearly enough time to build another engine to boost it back to a proper orbit.

Now there are riots everywhere. People stealing, robbing, and worse. Of course, they all blame me.

Even Jane.

The Neptune Fudge Affair

This was my third Tri-I assignment to Indigo 4. Invisible Intelligence Insertions were tricky. We only send in one at a time. Most operatives screwed up, either on the first one, or on their fourth or fifth mission. My drill sarge said they got sloppy after three. Sloppy operatives were never heard from again.

The war seemed pretty stagnant. The Indigs had the edge in speed and weapons; we seemed to be ahead of them on maneuverability, sensors, shields and tactics. And stealth.

Tri-I operatives were, well, invisible. Light, radio waves, radiation, all were unable to detect us. But we are not silent. Careful sensors can hear our breathing, even our heartbeats. Sonar, like bats on Old Earth, or calpods on Riga 4, can light us up real pretty. And, if we knocked a vase off of the mantle, it made noise when it crashed. Even in one-half G. We have to be careful. Always.

Indig society was very similar to ours. Military command structure was also pretty easy to figure out. And physically, Indigs looked a lot like humans, except they seem anorexic by Human standards. Their faces have recognizable eyes, ears, nose, and mouth. A long, thin body, two legs, two arms, no tails, but no hair, either. Contact with bodily fluids from an Indigo is fatal to Humans, after about four weeks of agonizing, degenerating health. Something about a self-replicating enzyme that eats

70

human mitochondria. Adult Indig stags were about eight feet tall, dames around seven. Neither wears any clothing. Ever. Indigo 4 stays about 31°C most of the time. Genitals seem the same. So, the skin, it's just like Human skin, except it's a deep, Day-Glo blue color. Our sarge said it was just like some kind of entertainers that never spoke in ancient times. I wouldn't know about that.

Anyway, my assignment was to collect whatever info I could from the Indig's Central Command. All I had to do was listen; for some reason, about 20% of Humans can read Indig's thoughts. The tricky part was picking out the thoughts of your target among all the other Indigs in about a 30 square meter area. Some one once told me it was a human reading Indig's thought that started the war, but I wouldn't know about that, either.

Anyway, I'm trailing my target over about two days, and I have his routines down pretty well. Up in time to wash and eat before sunrise, then off to the Command Central Complex. Mid-day meal at the Command Central Complex Cafeteria. Meetings, reports, committees all day long, then back home to his partner. I don't know if they 'get married' or anything like that. Evening meal, some entertainment, then sleep. Pretty boring.

Well, yesterday I follow the target, but mid afternoon he goes into a top security area. From his thoughts, I knew he would be there until he went home, so I decided to check out what his partner knew.

I stood outside the window of the food prep room, I think,

and watched her fuss around. Then she walks right at me! I checked my sys-op-rep, found my cloak was OK, and relaxed. Just a little. The Indig dame would have been a holo-model if she were a foot and a half shorter, and about 50 pounds heavier. Real cute, if you like long, thin, vertical eyes! Nice figure, too, for a Blue Skinny. Well, she is a General's partner!

She sets this shallow glass pan on the windowsill. Inside it is this shiny, light blue stuff. I can smell it: like chocolate, only a whole lot better. She waved her hand over it, like a cooling or wafting motion. That pan smelled really good. Her thoughts told me it was called "noptfud". From the color, I called it Neptune Fudge. It seemed to fit at the time.

I heard a noise, and noticed there was a baby in the room. Partner's thoughts told me it was the General's sister's kid, spending the day. She liked the baby, but was not too pleased with watching one that wasn't hers. It seemed the General was a trifle neglectful of his partner in the procreative department. She was concerned about his assistant; too pretty. Go figure.

I looked into her head for any news of upcoming offensives, extra stress on the General, things like that. Something may be coming up, but in the future. Not much there.

Just for kicks, I looked inside the baby. If you are telepathic, never look into a week-old baby!

Well, Partner takes baby to one of the spare sleeping chambers. I kept a thought-hold on her while I checked out the

Neptune Fudge. The smell of it brought out the feeling of walking into a bakery, or a candy store, or a Fair as a kid, even though the specific odor was sweet and wondrous, but totally new. It looked like fudge, light blue fudge. I shook the pan, and found it was nearly liquid; if I took some, it would fill in, resurface and no one could tell. So, I did. It tasted much better than it smelled. Sweet, bitter, chocolate-maple-molasses-caramel and something else that made it all work together. So, I took a little more.

General came home then, or I may have eaten the whole thing. Anyway, he had what I came for now; the Indigs were planning what General called an "all-or-nothing" simultaneous attack on our Fleet HQ, Senate Chambers, and Shipyards. No ships held back for defense. They were beginning the Armada formation in two weeks, and estimated they would be launching the three Armadas twelve weeks after that. They figured there was no way we could defend all three targets. Estimated travel to hit their targets was five weeks. That gave us fourteen weeks for me to get back, Fleet to assemble a strike group and then attack; we could send a small group to hit their Command Central Complex just after their three Armadas left, causing them to return and abort their attack. Without their Command Central Complex, they would listen to peace talks; the war could end quickly, and many lives could be saved on both sides.

As I made my way back to my ship, I caught the thoughts from the two. Back and forth about the baby, about the events of their respective days. Partner told General that the baby had made his first noptfud. They seemed excited about that, but Partner was upset that baby wasn't prepared properly, so she had a lot of clean up to do, and had not had a chance to dispose of the noptfud yet, so she had put it on the windowsill. Then the visual thought images hit me, right at the edge of my range; noptfud was poop. Indig baby poop! I ate Indig baby poop.

It was all I could do to not vomit all over the General's front lawn. That would give me away by sight and sound! I hurried back to my concealed ship, fighting to keep the vile blue goo down the whole way. At last I came to a safe spot, next to my ship, and let it come up. Blue vomit with blood streaks is not a pretty sight.

It took me a minute or so to get enough strength to get in the ship. It took several more to get enough energy to take off. My ship has no communications gear, as that would defeat the invisibility system. I should have just hit the self-destruct; my trip home will take five weeks. I'll be dead in four.

Because I got sloppy.

What Goes Around

The harvest meeting began today. I have high hopes for it. If I can sell my invention, perhaps Jasmine's father will allow us to marry.

Each year, people came from all over, by land and by sea, carrying their goods, packed upon the backs of beasts. It seems all roads and all winds lead to Thimesqes. I've made a good living here, working with wood and stone. But Jasmine's father says she is worthy of a higher class than I. So, I must sell my invention this year, before Cirqsees pays Jasmine's dowry.

Long and hard have I worked on this. Never has one thing held so much promise to better our world than my simple little invention! All I have to do now is convince some one of that. Someone with money.

I keep my invention out of sight. I have made four of them, the better number to sell to a rich man. I cannot afford to lose them!

My invention will change everything about our way of life; the beasts carrying goods will move ten times as much, twice as fast. Water will grind grain, and weave cloth. It will make clay vessels uniform and with fine lines. It can make an army so fast as to be invincible. There is no limit as to what it can do!

I only hope I can convince a rich man of the worth of the

thing. Tomorrow will tell. I've named it after myself, so that after tomorrow, the world will know it was changed by my invention.

Tomorrow the world will know of me, Wheel.

The Sisyphus Gene

Joseph shook his head as he walked through the long, bleak passage cut into the ancient walls of the Temple. Everything he had studied, the entire Order of Divine Interstellar Exploration, every policy, every procedure, every training seminar, every performance audit, and every safety poster had been designed to prevent this very thing from ever happening again. And yet, it had. And Joseph knew, as his footsteps echoed off of the cold, grey stone of the hallway, this was information that had to be delivered quickly, and in person. Preparations had to be made, after all.

Although he had attended early school with him, Joseph had never been to the Office of The Father of Species Studies before. He reasoned that this would be the only time he would ever be here. Such events as he was reporting happened once in, well, Creation.

He found himself studying the ancient wood of the door, thinking of what to say, of how to begin his report, for several moments. Joseph decided the best approach was to just get it over with. He made a quick wish and pressed the buzzer.

The door vanished and Joseph entered. Silently the door again sealed the reception room.

"May I help you, Brother?" sang the pleasant voice of the receptionist.

"Joseph of Dal Raitha 4, with an urgent report for The Father."

"Father Albert is expecting you, Joseph. You have made good time. Nothing too terrible, I hope?"

Joseph's expression unconsciously betrayed that he was not amused by her joke. If she only knew, he thought. But, then, he thought to himself, she could do nothing about it if she did!

The receptionist's expression had darkened considerably as she pressed her intercom and announced in a pale voice, "B-brother Joseph is h-here, Father." She looked up at Joseph and whispered through tearing eyes, "You may enter, Brother. And may God be with you."

"And with you. Always." Joseph returned the hope with genuine kindness.

The office struck Joseph as small for the importance of the title, yet large enough, and appropriately equipped, to handle the required bureaucracy. The bureaucracy that Joseph knew had failed, as it eventually had throughout all of recorded history, and at least one Creation before that.

"Joseph. I wish I could say it is good to see you, and all the other pleasant small talk greeting one enjoys exchanging with old friends too long removed. Please, be seated. May I get you something?" Father Albert motioned to the small, 6-person conference table to Joseph's left. The Father had, of course, tracked his former schoolmate's travel here. There was only one thing to report in person rather than by virtual link.

"Thank you, Father Albert. If I may, water would be nice." Joseph replied as he sat in the nearest chair at the conference table.

"Call me Al, Jo. No sense for titles here. Ice? No? Here. Now, just tell me what happened, my old friend."

"Intelligent species 12-673-892.661," Joseph sighed. "Located fairly far out in a spiral arm of galaxy 334, quadrant 2, sector 12b." Joseph began in a professional, but subdued, resigned tone. "My Section Head did his required interview with the standard last example, and called me in as soon as he suspected the problem. I conducted my interview in person, as I was only 7 galaxies away, and could get there within a few minutes."

"Go on." Al set the water down in front of Jo as he took the seat next to him.

"Al, when I asked it about God, she knew."

"What exactly did she say, Jo?"

Joseph took a big breath, then let it out slowly before continuing, "I asked her if she knew how the universe was created. She said, 'God created Heaven and Earth in 6 days. On the seventh day, God rested.' They called their planet Earth, Al."

Al sat back heavily into the dark leather padding of his chair. "Yes. Is that all?"

"Next I asked which god created the universe. She replied that there is only one true God. When I asked her who created her kind, she told me that God created a male, and from his rib, created.... A female."

Al felt the tears begin, and fought a losing battle against them. "Then?" he whispered.

Jo choked a little, trying to control the vast emotions boiling to escape, but managed to continue, "She told that God had given the male and female reign over all the creatures and all the resources of the Earth, and of the oceans, and of the skies, but that God had forbidden certain knowledge to the male and female, but that the female had been beguiled by the serpent and then the male by the female, so that they had eaten of the tree of knowledge. And God had cast them from the paradise of the garden of Creation."

Jo stopped and took a sip of water, then a more substantial swallow before continuing, "Then she, she told me, Oh, God! Why!" Joseph sobbed for a time. When he had recovered, he began again, "She told me that in time the world had too much sin, and so The Son of God was sent to suffer for their sins! He spoke of loving one another, of doing what was right, of being kind and just. The Son of God was tortured, and crucified upon a cross, for their sins! Oh, Al, it's all my fault! Had I been a better supervisor...."

"Jo, relax. We need to know where our procedures failed, so

we can tell the next ones how to do better the next time. Have you any idea how we missed this?"

"T-they w-were a close, a perfect morphological match for the Species 1, but that-that's not unusual, about a third of intelligent species are. It was the genetics. My sector delayed the testing due to a lab fire. By the time we found out they were over 99.999% identical to Species 1, we had already ended all but the last female. As I was interviewing her, she told me that The Son of God had assured her of eternal life in Him. Then she closed her eyes and died. Al, we need to start the Ark now. When it is finished, God will select the people...."

"I know, Joseph. I know. We have destroyed God's chosen yet again. Why are we always unworthy, no matter the precautions we take?"

Father Albert rose, walked to his desk, and opened a locked drawer. He removed a small, brown box, and opened the cover. Reaching inside, he pressed the button there. Through the open window, they heard the alarms sound seven times, and each knew that the alarms were repeated on every planet and ship, as each of their kind prepared for The End of Creation.

"This Creation will be destroyed in 12 weeks. We will have that long to build an Ark that will survive the destruction of the universe, using God's plans, handed down from our ancestors who had found the species we discovered and wrongfully eliminated 4,652 Creations ago. We know this universe will end in 12 weeks, so we will select the best of us, the life from our world, with all the cultural, genetic, and technological information we possess, to ride the Ark, until God creates a new universe. They will resume our civilization then in the new Creation."

"I should go then, and begin uploading the databases. May I?" Joseph gestured at the window.

"Good idea, flying will save time. Godspeed, my friend."

"God be with you, Albert." Joseph replied as he spread his leathery wings and flew out of the window.

Father Albert sighed heavily, wrapping his wings tightly around his long, slimy body. "If they are worthy, and can manage to eliminate only the harmful species that God does not choose, while sparing the chosen species, then, in the next universe, perhaps The Son of God will appear and give *them* the gift of everlasting life."

Whatever It Takes

They call me "The Negotiator."

I've negotiated peaceful trade on seventeen different worlds. Some say, that because of me, there has been peace in the Galaxy over the last fifty years. Hey, if the shoe fits.....

Take this assignment, for example. The Goltz are a race of mammal-like omnivores from near Cygnus. We're at a seemingly insurmountable impasse right now.

The Goltz have a lot of consumers, are interested in a lot of our products, and have many minerals and ores we would love to get at reasonable prices. But they drive a hard bargain.

So my job is to find that one thing that The Goltz want and can't get anywhere else.

Extensive research goes into finding that product. I've spent over three years on Goltz Prime finding it. In the end, it came to me at lunch, yesterday.

Walking down the 'Main Drag,' as my dad would have called it, in the capitol of Goltz Prime, I noticed dozens of vendors selling lunch from carts. Hey, some things are universal. I bought some street-vendor lunch.

It was good. No hiding that. But it was also familiar, to some extent. Except for one thing; the sausage-like product needed garlic. Desperately.

So, I made a call home, and had a package delivered.

That package arrived today. The meeting this morning was designed for one purpose only; to keep The Goltz delegation interested until lunch. Hollywood is good at that, so I showed them movies. With that, I succeeded.

So, we broke for lunch at 12:45. I invited The Goltz Delegation to stay and enjoy a typical Earth lunch. With great fanfare the servers brought in the spectacular spread: Hot Dogs.

Hoffman's Hot Dogs, to be specific. Straight from Earth. With fresh buns and bright yellow Heinz mustard.

The hotdogs were gone by 1:15PM. We signed the trade agreement at 1:20PM.

Everything Happens For A Reason

The door burst open as the huge alien warrior stormed into the vestibule. Most of Washington D.C. was under alien control by now, the third day of the invasion. Heavy fighting may still remain, but this building should prove no great obstacle. The warrior had almost felt insulted at the assignment.

Stanley Beamish sat at his desk, absorbed by his work. While he took note of the commotion raised by the warrior's entrance, it was not enough to distract him from his assigned duties until he had completed the page before him. The Agency depended upon him, and hundreds like him, completing this paperwork. It was what drove the bureaucracy, after all; paperwork was their only real product.

The warrior pointed his huge plasma cannon menacingly at Stanley and growled in the voice that had always produced a satisfying quiver among the conquered. Stanley simply coughed, "Hrumpf!"

"You will surrender to the Kardroic Horde!" shouted the warrior.

Stanley never looked up, but spun his wheeled office chair about and opened a file cabinet behind him. With great, careful, and extremely slow deliberation he removed a two-inch pile of forms from it. Slowly, deliberately, and with decided indifference

Stanley handed the forms to the huge warrior before him.

"Fill these out, in triplicate, and get them notarized. Then bring them back to the seventeenth floor, section L-12A. Ask for Alice Higginbottom. Leave the forms with her. Don't forget to complete the 'return address' form, 9-12A.45.79C. You should have a reply within twelve to fourteen business days."

The invasion seemed to stop in its tracks near the end of day three.

Ten days later, the alien invasion was officially declared repulsed.

The City

The objective was within the city center before him. He began the easy trot into the city even as he scanned the files for the appropriate disguise.

C-47L moved at over 400 meters per second with minimal effort; he had been designed for a mission such as this. His processors shed excess heat as he ran through thousands of variations to find the optimal plan of action; his mission was to eliminate the target. Simple. Direct. Brutal.

Taking the external form of a parcel delivery employee, C-47L slowed to a speed mimicking the walking speed of the local population. This was going to be a very easy assignment, he postulated as he entered the huge Central Planning Tower.

He moved efficiently to the elevation shafts, and indicated the 97th floor as his destination. Security bought his disguise without question. He smiled to himself.

C-47L once was John Adams, a human escort from Bermuda. Poor decisions had placed him in debt to some unethical people. Eventually, after much more pain than he cared to remember, he ended up as the driving intelligence for this cyborg assassin. Once this mission was over, they told him, he would be free again.

The door to the suite opened before him, and C-47L scanned the room; there was only one person there, and his circuits told him it was his target.

John stared at the young woman in front of him; tall, slim, and blonde. She smiled at the human appearance of a deliveryman, waiting for her package. This was where C-47L was supposed to hand over the explosive package; John hesitated. He knew this woman. He had met her a year ago in a Georgetown nightclub. She was kind and pleasant. He never tried to charge her for that night. Or any of the next three.

His programming now demanded he hand her the package, but John fought it, pulling back, searching for the override he knew was there...

The President's daughter watched in horror as the delivery man blew up before her.

The Last One

I can hear it, moving around outside the cave. Why did I pick *this* cave to hide in? The opening is too big, it can get in!

I am pretty sure that I'm the last one. I've received no communications in over two weeks now. The creatures hunt us down and kill us. It is the end of everything.

It's moving again; I can hear the clattering metal of its suit. I have so little left to fight with. My flamer is empty, and there is nothing near here to reload it with. I have not eaten since…a long time, yes.

Once we were a great culture. We had families, hopes, dreams, art, music, love. Then they came and spread like a cancer across the land, killing us off, one by one, planting their food everywhere. They pushed us further and further north, into climates too cold to sustain us. But we tried. We wanted to live.

We finally fought back, as best we could. But we simply were not equipped to defeat them. Oh, we made them pay dearly for every one of us they killed. Very dearly. For a time, it looked like we had won a kind of truce. But it did not last.

And now, I am the last one.

Legend has it that in the remote past, we traveled the stars, marveling at the wonders and the vastness of all creation.

Somehow we lost that, and all of us ended up here, on this little ball of rock, water and sand. We met the killers here. At first, they welcomed us. They called us angels from heaven. We taught them how to work metal, build with stone, and to govern justly.

And then, one day, they started killing us. Now, we are no more. I am the last one, of that I am certain.

It is moving again, creeping closer. I can hear its metal suit grating on the rocks as it slinks through the cave. It wants but to kill me, it has declared as much, in a loud, boastful voice. And, I am very weary. You see, I am old now, for my kind, and I would not see the next spring even in happier times. So, the savage in the metal suit will find me, and kill me. But I will not give up life's last breath without a fight, feeble as it may be!

There, the noise, closer! Death comes! Oh, creation, I do not wish to pass from thy warm embrace into that cold, dark, loneliness beyond! Why must we all be killed in such an inglorious, brutal manner? Death, have you no heart?

There! I see it now. Light glints off of the metal suit. I have managed to kill one before, but it cost me an arm. And my family. Those metal suits, they are too strong for our weapons!

Except for the flamer. That terrifies these terrors! They run from it, but only to return again to slaughter us.

It's closer. I am frightened. I think of Jorrelle, my mate; the most beautiful Jorrelle! How her tears flowed when they found our home and they butchered our children! I cannot bare the thoughts of what those lives could have been! Jorrelle! My love! She died as much from a broken heart as from the blows of the savages! Jorrelle! Forgive me, for I have failed you!

Here! The battle joined, you worthless, immoral abomination!

Struck! Pain! Lash out, again! Again! I've landed a good blow!

Pain! Pain upon pain upon pain piercing pain! Darkness closing in!

The savage is talking. No! I don't wish to pass hearing those boisterous words!

Jorrelle! It said it had killed me, the last Dragon!

I am sorry, so sorry, Jorrelle!

While You Are Waiting...

"Miss, do you have any idea how much longer it will be? I'm losing time from work..."

"Your name will be called when it's your turn," Miss orange-hair didn't even look up from her computer screen.

"With all the advancements in modern technology, society, and civilization, you would think the 'waiting room' would have been obsolete by now."

"Hmm. Sure, I guess." Orange-hair looked up and past me, "Next!"

She wasn't rude. Not really. And I may have been just a little...insistent.

"Look, I've been waiting since 9:45. I had a 10 o'clock appointment. It's almost noon now! I'm just asking, how much longer?"

Brown eyes glared at me from between horned rim glasses and orange hair. I sighed and went back to my seat.

I made the appointment two weeks ago. Usually, I'll make these for Saturdays, but this week was a holiday and the place would be closed. I rationalized it, thinking I could be in and out in an hour or so.

Now I've lost the whole morning's pay.

I looked at orange-hair again. The 'next' went back to his seat, so I went back up.

"Miss, please, I need to tell my boss what time I'll be back."

"Mr. Harris," she let out a sigh between chomps on her gum, "I can't say what time they'll be ready for you. The best I can do is give you a complimentary virdistrack to pass the time while you are waiting." She pushed a chipcard towards me.

" Yeah, um…" I took it. I don't usually go in for virtual reality distractions, but I had nothing better to do. Back at my seat, I slid the chipcard into the slot in the armrest.

I should have read the title.

I felt a little dizzy until the lights came up.

When my eyes adjusted to the bright orange light, I just felt scared.

Knowing that a virdistrack isn't real doesn't matter. Every sense you have tells you it is.

The energy field put out by the chair paralyzes your voluntary muscles, so you don't go running around the waiting room. If you did manage to stand up, the virdistrack ends as soon as you're out of the energy field.

I tried to stand up. I just rose up inside the illusion.

Bad move.

It saw me now. I could see it walking towards me, claws snapping like a barber clicking his scissors.

It must have been seven feet high at the top of its shell. The four claws were each about three feet long. The four legs didn't move very fast, but they managed to move the Arachny along at about 10 miles per hour.

I had about 90 seconds.

A quick look around didn't help. There were two dozen Arachnys surrounding me, each one busy devouring a Soleo, the ten-foot long olive green slugs that are the primary prey of the Arachny.

I looked down at my hands.

Except, I didn't have any. All I could see was a thick leathery skin covered with slimy goo.

Great. I was a Soleo.

I tried running.

Undulating is not a particularly fast locomotive technique.

My fear began to rise. The Arachny was closer. A lot closer.

I could smell it, a strong fishy odor. A shiver ran from my head down to my...the end of the slug.

Wet. I felt wetter now. Something heavy was on my back. I turned my head to look.

The slime was oozing out of my skin. Gallons of it, thick and slippery, yet sticky at the same time.

And it smelled like rotten eggs.

But I knew it wouldn't matter. Aranchys can't smell.

It was on me now. A claw snipped near my ear. Another next to my eye stalk.

I knew the end was near.

"There, Mr. Harris! How do you like that?"

I looked in the mirror.

"Fine, as always Max. Here you go, and keep the change!" I handed max the twenty and ran my hand over my freshly cut hair, taking a whiff of the tonic Max used.

"Thank you Mr. H!"

I glanced at my watch and then waved at Miss Orange-hair as I walked out of the barbershop.

I checked the clock over my cubicle.

10:25.

I only had to write three more virtutracks before lunch to make my quota.

The Used Car Salesman

Here is the little red beauty right here. Ye-up, it's a '58.
The story behind it? Sure.

I guess being well off has its perks. Yes, I do own a mansion and a yacht. Oh, it was difficult to get to this point, believe me. Double jobs, long hours, cultivated professional relationships, and careful investments. It all paid off. It was a great plan, but I can't take credit for it. It was her plan, our plan. Just as our goals came within reach, she disappeared. No note, no clues, no money withdrawals, no possessions taken, just vanished.

So, two years later, feeling anything but normal, I found myself at the point where my money did all the work, and I could be very comfortable, if not happy. That is how I happened to be driving along Interstate 40, just west of Santa Rosa, New Mexico, at twilight. Twenty-plus miles of flat, straight pavement under the wheels of my custom '58 T-Bird.

This is not just any '58 T-Bird. Custom. It looks stock, but under that elegant late '50s styling was a modern muscle car. Power everything; steering, brakes, windows, seats, top. AC. A sound system you could open a nightclub with. Power, yeah; 900 plus horses under that simple, bright, shiny, red hood scoop. Run to the back by a 4 speed racing tranny, with a dual rear end that lets you go from dragstrip to road racer instantly. And, in white outlined navy cursive script under the side mirror, you'll see "Emily; L'il Heartbreaker." Yeah, I know, move on, closure, all that. Let's just say it was therapeutic. Under her name, the crests of all the Lamborghinis, Porches, Ferraris, Cobras, Dodges, Corvettes, and Jags Emily had broken the hearts of. Count 'em; 37 in all. There's even a Maybach emblem there, one Emily splashed on The Autobahn.

Anyway, I had pretty much been spending all my time going as fast as possible in this car. So, I'm cruisin' west down the highway at about 150 or so, hardtop on; you do not want bugs hitting your face at over a hundred! So, I'm enjoying the colors of a gorgeous sky just after sunset, watching the stars show up as the daylight faded out. I had driven eastward earlier, checking for speed traps, and found the road clear. No it was time for that rush that made me forget her, for a few minutes, at least. Driving 20 miles in less than five minutes can do that. Sometimes.

That's when I saw the lights off to the south. Streaks of multi-colored lights leading down to a green glow, about ten miles off road. I had just happened to glance that way, and saw them appear, just like a switch was thrown.

So, I slow down and see a trail leading from the road off in the direction of these lights. Yeah, I took it. It was surprisingly even and easy to drive on, but you couldn't see it unless the light hit it just right.

About ten miles off the highway, the road goes up just a bit, and I'm looking down on, well, you won't believe this, but it was there; three big, really big, ships. No, not Navy ships. Though, each was about the size of an aircraft carrier. Space ships! One round, like a puffy version of a 1950's movie flying saucer, one long and pointed at both ends, and one like a rounded triangle.

But the space ships were not the strangest thing there. The green glow came from a floating strip, like lights for a baseball stadium, but floating in air. Beneath the lights was pavement. A mile long strip of flat, straight pavement, like it had been burned and polished into the desert. And at one end, three cars!

Well, cars are the best description I could think of. They each had wheels and clear windows in front, and some kind of pipes out the back. Three different designs, each a different color and shape. So, being a curious guy, and feeling I had little to lose, I drove down the trail to the end of the road.

My arrival caused considerable agitation, I can tell you. There were three different shapes of aliens walking around; one a short, stocky, green type I named Toads in my head; another a tall, grey, thin pasty kind I call the Zombies, and the last, a type shaped just like us, but covered in what looked like a winding of cloth. The Mummies. As I drove up, the twenty or so aliens that were busy moving things around all stopped what they were doing and stared at me. When I stopped, they all went back to work, except for this one Zombie who looked like a ten year old Ronnie Howard stretched to nine feet tall, who glided over to me.

Yeah, glided; his legs just hung down as he moved, feet about two inches off the ground.

Well, Zombie-boy starts clacking at me. All clicks, clacks, and clucks. When I look at him like he's from Mars, he starts over again, whistling some noise like Chinese-Arabic-Russian through a flute. So, I said, "What?"

That seemed to help Ronnie, who replied in a sort of French accent, "Race or watch?" That's when I noticed the grandstands off to the side of the strip. There must have been a couple of thousand aliens sitting there.

"I'll race." I shrugged. Ronnie motioned me to the closest end of the pavement, near two of the cars. One was lime green, a rounded Jello-mold contraption, the other an orange needle. They sat side-by-side behind a line on the strip, with a bright blue light floating in front of them. I watched the light turn from blue to red, and both cars made a lot of noise and a lot of smoke, and took off down the track, tires screeching. Counting in my head, I guessed these were pretty close to my T-Bird in speed. It would be a good test for Emily; who's heart would she break tonight?

I watched as part of the crowd cheered, at least I think it was a cheer, and the two cars cruised back to the starting line. The side of the Orange Needle opened and a Zombie climbed out, made a gesture to the Jello mold, and then motioned to a group of Zombies near some equipment. One of them walked out leading a nice looking horse, saddle and all, and handed the reins to Toad that had climbed out of the Jello mold. The Toad jumped up and down for a minute, and then was swarmed by a dozen or so other Toads. After about 90 seconds of celebration, they broke up. Some Toads led the horse up a ramp into the saucer-ship, and the others started working on the Jello mold.

Just then Ronnie motioned me to the starting line. OK, I had this pretty well figured out, except what to give them if I lost.

I sat at the starting line, and the Orange Needle pulls up beside me. That thing was pretty loud up close, while my Ford was still in "street-quiet" mode, as I liked to listen to music when I raced. I had a Beach Boys cars mix on tonight. I watched the light; there was nothing to time. It changed to red as "Fun, Fun, Fun" poured out of my speakers, and I floored it as I let out the clutch. I just let the Ford do the work, and concentrated on shifting smoothly. Up ahead, I saw a red line of light across the track, getting closer fast. When I went through it, I glanced at my speedometer-182, not too shabby-and at the Orange Needle. He was a good 50 yards behind me.

Well, I followed him back to the starting area, and got out. He was already out, and gestured to me. And I'm thinking, what would I do with a horse? But out comes a Zombie with a happy-looking Golden Retriever on a leash! So, after rejecting naming the dog Emily, I named her Leia and sat her in the passenger seat.

Back at the starting line, I saw the Jello mold line up next to a silver wedge. It was hard to see from where I was, but it looked real close at the finish. Again, the cheers from the crowd told me the Toad won again.

When I looked to see his prize, I nearly collapsed. My knees went weak, my head spun; the Mummy led a woman over to the Toad. It was a gorgeous freckle-faced strawberry-blonde that looked just like, it WAS Emily! My Emily! She glanced at me, and I saw her eyes light up! She was led up that ramp before I could react, but I knew what I needed to do.

The race with the Mummy's Wedge was a little closer, but I still smoked him by 15 yards. My prize was an enthusiastic black Labrador Retriever. I named him Luke, and he politely sat in the back, behind Leia.

So, here I am, the only time I've ever been nervous with this car before a race. Me, the two dogs, and my music at the starting line, next to the Jello mold. I switched Emily to Racing Mode, and the un-muffled sounds of that big engine drew what I want to believe were sounds of awe from the crowd. I maxed the volume on my music, and heard "Baby when you race today, just take along my love with you" as the light changed.

I really don't remember the race itself. Everything after Emily came down that ramp and into my arms just sort of dissolved away.

Well, anyway, that's the story behind her. She's the Official

Universal Drag Racing Champ, and here is the trophy to prove it. Diamonds? Well, I never thought to read the appraisal, just looked at the number on the bottom of the form. You can't find another car like her, and I think $2.5 mil is a very reasonable price. I believe Emily has poured some champagne for us in the den. I'll break out a couple of Belinda Empires to seal the deal. This way.

Why are we selling it? We're moving to Kokomo; no drag strips there! And, from the challenges I keep getting... well, I'm just tired of all those races. I'm running out of space to keep my winnings!

The trophy? No, the trophy's not included. That I'm keeping.

Luke! Leia! Down! Excuse the dogs, they're friendly, but enthusiastic. That? Oh, the other race I won. It's called a "Druck"; we named it "Han". Perfectly harmless. Gets along great with the dogs. You've never seen a three-foot long flying reptile before, have you?

I hope you enjoyed my stories. If you did, please leave a review on Amazon and tell others about it.

About James W. McAllister

I founded Fortiter Publishing LLC in November 2013 as a vehicle to get all these great Science Fiction and Fantasy stories out of my head.

"FORTITER" is inscribed on the MacAlister Clan Crest. The word means "to go forward, boldly." I am grateful for the Clan Chief's permission to use the Crest and Tartan in my company's logo, and to use "FORTITER" in my company's name.

I have been interested in science fiction since reading the Lensmen Series of books by E. E. "Doc" Smith in Junior High School. TV shows like Star Trek and Battlestar Galactica, and movies such as Robinson Crusoe on Mars and Star Wars further peaked my interest in the genre.

See my Amazon Author's page here:

http://amazon.com/author/jwmcallister

Other books by James W. McAllister

STARCLAN Book I

THE TURRET

Starclan Foundation

STARCLAN Book II

THE BEST LAID PLANS

Birth of the Starclan

STARCLAN Book III

A MATTER OF HONOR

Starclan Chrysalis

Coming 2016

STAGED FRIGHT

A John Martin Adventure

RODS

Another John Martin Adventure